GRAMPY

A Novella

By

Bonnie Benhayon

© 2024 Bonnie Benhayon. All rights reserved.

This book is a work of fiction. Any names, characters, companies, organizations, places, events, locales, and incidents are either used in a fictitious manner or are fictional. Any resemblance to actual persons, living or dead, actual companies or organizations, or actual events is purely coincidental.

This book is dedicated to my husband, Peter, for his unwavering love and support of my interest in writing, and to my daughter, Jocelyn, for her spot-on, unvarnished feedback.

Special thanks to Robin Koval for the cover art and Vicky Haygood for editing.

CONTENTS

Proverb

Chapter 1:	Meet the Family	9
Chapter 2:	Allegra	21
Chapter 3:	Amber	35
Chapter 4:	Vivian	47
Chapter 5:	Gigi	59
Chapter 6:	Margeaux	69
Chapter 7:	Suzy	77
Chapter 8:	Sarah	85
Chapter 9:	Athena	89
Chapter 10:	The End	97
Postscript		114
Notes		118

Looks can be deceiving

- Proverb

Meet the Family

I had just turned ten when I overheard a vicious argument between my mother and a man I didn't know in the back garden of our house in Washington, DC. At one point the man began to shout, which made it possible for me to hear him more clearly through the open windows of the sunroom, where I was curled up on a pile of pillows with a book about Scottish castles. The man's main point was that my parents and everyone in our family were terrible people.

At this time in my life, I still unconditionally adored and trusted my parents. Approval from my glamorous, hard-charging mother and my introverted and Nordically handsome father was always at the forefront of my thoughts. My therapists have all said that this is because they were both stingy with their time and attention.

My mother has always been consumed by her work and her need for Grampy's attention. My father, the author of a series of best-selling murder mysteries solved by a Swedish rowing coach, was either locked in his office writing or deep in thought, devising plot twists or new storylines. I'm not sure either of them actually like children. They live in a very adult world full of business deals, politics, media appearances, and their respective work. My brother and I were granted more access to them when we finally entered adulthood, but by then it was too late. The idea of parents as confidants or someone you would just hang with had been snuffed out long before we received our first invitation to one of their parties or our formal assignments in the family businesses. Our parents were more like our bosses. Their boss was Grampy.

When I overheard that argument as a child, I had thought it was an opportunity for me to impress my mother, so I ran outside and confronted the angry man. I stood my ground and defended my family, firmly telling him that my parents were wonderful, really wonderful. Everyone loved them. Everyone wanted to know everything about them because they were so wonderful. At ten, that's why I thought photographers were always following them around; I think that's how my parents explained their presence on our doorstop every morning. Now I know my parents had a team of people devoted to keeping them in the media every day.

I remember the angry man trying to placate me and saying that he was sure I loved my parents very much and that they loved me very much. Then he asked me if my parents were teaching me about right and wrong and making the world a better place. I remember he looked at my mother even though he was asking me the question. I confidently replied, "Yes, it's the golden rule! It's all about the business. Take care of the family business and the business will take care of the family."

He gave my mother a look that I now recognize as disgust, then patted me on the head and left. My mother was silent and showed no emotion until the man was gone. I remember the silence starting to make me feel worried that I had done something wrong.

Once the man was gone, my mother knelt down and gave me a tight hug. She told me that I was her fierce little warrior princess, and I was ecstatic. Then she said something that she would say to me repeatedly throughout my life: "Allegra, there are some things we only say out loud when we are with family. What you said today about our golden rule is one of those things. Always remember to be very, very careful about what you say to people outside our family."

She smiled radiantly, focused completely on me. The sun at her back made her look like she was glowing. Her perfectly highlighted, honey-colored hair and her shimmery green silk blouse enhanced the effect. My mother always dresses in jewel tones. They are bold, distinctive, and make a statement: she won't be ignored. In that moment, she was the most beautiful thing I had ever seen. I hugged her very hard until she had to gently push me away to take a call from Grampy.

I learned soon after that incident that *our* golden rule is not *the* golden rule. Our family isn't big on religion and church, though we've all been photographed at famous cathedrals, temples, and mosques at one time or another.

If it wasn't for Grampy, you could dismiss us as just another self-absorbed rich family living above the logistical inconveniences of everyday life most people face. But when the incident with the angry man happened, Grampy was President of the United States and my mother worked with him in the White House.

Eighteen months later, Grampy failed to win reelection. Six months after his decisive defeat, he had a stroke at the family estate in Bridgehampton and died instantly. My mother and Uncle Jamie tried to mount a huge, week-long funeral to celebrate Grampy's contributions to the country, but the new president was having none of it. A state funeral, with Grampy lying in state at the Capitol

Building and flags flying at half-staff, was fine; the new president would even speak at the funeral. But no funds for a monument on the national mall, no immediate renaming of a federal building, and no to the ambitious list of other grandiose requests. Grampy's successor wasn't sure the country was as heartbroken as my mother claimed over the death of a former president who barely won 30 percent of the popular vote in his final election.

After Grampy's death, his widow and fourth wife, Amber, moved to London with her twins, Chance and Thorne. They were named after soap opera characters from a show she watched with her mother and her aunt when she was growing up. She did not stay in touch with our family after she moved and she never speaks publicly about Grampy.

Like all of Grampy's wives, Amber grew up poor, which made it easier to get them to sign prenups that gave them relatively nothing in the event of a divorce. Amber got lucky when Grampy was elected president: she was able to renegotiate. She limited her FLOTUS duties to two joint appearances per month and one appearance on her own. She also had to hold his hand when they walked across the lawn to the helicopter. Her clothing, jewelry, and personal grooming budgets were dramatically increased. She could go back to New York on her own every other month, and if Grampy embarrassed her in public, her payout was increased by a lot.

Grampy's first wife, Gigi, is my maternal grandmother. He met my Yaya when he was in college in a small town in upstate New York. She was a townie with an exotic, dark beauty and an irresistible laugh—the kind of laugh that is contagious even if you hadn't heard the joke. It was a minor scandal in the family because he "married down" but by all accounts, she is the one wife Grampy truly loved. They were married for almost twenty years and had two children: my uncle, Jonathan, and my mom, Vivian. Until his dying day, Grampy still carried a picture of Yaya in his wallet, and he sent her jewelry every year on her birthday. It wasn't a bitter divorce, but it was crushing for my grandmother and she never remarried. She once told me she was a one-man woman—she is very old school like that.

Grampy grew up in a socially prominent and wealthy New York family. When he took over the family business, he expanded it into a global transportation company which launched us into a stratospheric level of wealth. We are one of the largest privately held companies in the world, and Grampy and my mother were always included in those lists of the world's richest people. My mother still is.

 After the divorce, Grampy bought an airline and he met Suzy the Stew, who became wife number two. He had this marriage annulled immediately. No one will say why, and even during the campaign it never came out. Reporters and biographers have tried to uncover the story, but Suzy the Stew has kept her mysterious secret.

 Next came Margeaux. Her real name was Mary Margaret but she was an actress and thought Margeaux was more original and sophisticated. My mother said Margeaux had big pageant hair and was very "showy" when she was married to Grampy. Their marriage lasted for nine years, during which my other uncle, Jamieson, was born, and Grampy stepped away from the family business to become a TV star. He hosted a reality show about what it takes to be a CEO. In those days, his cutting comments were considered humorous and his merciless on-screen critiques were thought to be insightful and praised universally as a demonstration of his superior business acumen. I've watched old recordings and, personally, I think Grampy was simply mean. Cruelty was at the heart of his humor.

There were lots of beautiful young women around and he moved on from Margeaux. One good thing you can say about Grampy is that he wasn't a cheater; he liked a clean break. After the divorce, Margeaux became the signature character for a long-running series of insurance ads, married an orthodontist, and is living happily in her home state of California.

Finally, there was Amber. She grew up in a trailer park in West Virginia. She was truly drop-dead gorgeous, an old-time movie star-style beauty à la Grace Kelly. Amber came to New York at sixteen to model and she made an okay living at it, though it was clear after a few years that she would not attain supermodel status. When Grampy decided he wanted to go into politics, he determined he needed a photogenic wife on his arm and discreet inquiries were made on his behalf. Her modeling agency set them up.

It took months to negotiate the prenup, as Amber wanted a child but Grampy was already a grandfather and he thought it might make him look ridiculous. Amber prevailed and, during the primaries, gave birth to fraternal twins. What Grampy loved best about the twins was the media coverage of him as a doting father and the less-than-subtle references to his continued virility. Off camera, he rarely saw the boys. When he was in a bad mood, he told Amber he wasn't even sure they were his sons because they were conceived via in vitro fertilization.

Almost from birth, my brother, cousins, and I were assigned future roles in the family that directed us down specific paths. Chad would follow in our mother's footsteps and lead the businesses and our cousin Jonny would be his backup. I was originally assigned the backup role, but I was rerouted to the family foundation in my teenage years. Athena was always beautiful, literally from the moment she was born—she even started life with a full head of her signature jet-black hair—so she was chosen as the "face" of our generation.

It was also expected that we would stay on course and in character at all times, especially in public. We were groomed accordingly.

As planned, my brother Chad was sporty and preppy—an All-American bro and an overachiever. He won trophy after trophy at St. Paul's and graduated near the top of his class. His success continued at Yale and Columbia. He's a golden child like our mother, with the square-jawed, Nordic good looks of our father.

My cousin Jonny is following in his father's footsteps and is apprenticing to be the backup for Chad. Jonny is musical, like his mother, but acquiesced early on to his father's insistence on a career in the family businesses. He seems satisfied with his second-banana role, but his real passion isn't the company; it's his new husband Jorge and their show dogs. He's probably the most grounded of all us, but it's a low bar.

I'm an introvert like my father and I didn't want to go into the businesses. I wanted to be a philosophy professor and spend my life on some beautiful Gothic campus debating the writing of Plato, Descartes, Kant, and even Machiavelli. My mother dismissed this idea as unacceptable no matter how many ways I tried to make the case. When college loomed on the horizon, it was decided I could be the philanthropic one and run the family foundation. I would still major in business, but was allowed a minor in philosophy. The price for my small victory was to stay in New York during my college years—no picturesque New England campus for me—plus required weekly dinners at home. Like Jonny, I acquiesced to the wishes of my strong-willed parent. My official bio says I am relentlessly dedicated to giving back to society and that I've had this calling since childhood.

My cousin Athena headed to Georgetown to study International Relations and break a lot of hearts. After graduation, she joined me at the foundation with a special focus on Grampy's presidential library. Her days and nights are filled with fundraisers and galas that provide opportunities for her to be photographed. I know she is unhappy being relegated to such a superficial role. She'd never say it and she defuses any tension between us with humor, but I can see it in her face and feel it in every interaction we have. Her role is to bring glamor to the family's image with her sultry good looks, but she is capable of and wants much more than to be pigeonholed in this way. If I were describing Athena, I'd call her the ambitious one. Unlike Jonny, she won't settle into a role as anyone's backup for the rest of her life—especially not mine.

Allegra

We had more or less forgotten about Chance and Thorne over the years—they were almost never mentioned by anyone in the family or the media—when they sent me a message asking to talk to me about the family foundation. The boys would be eighteen in the spring, and that meant they automatically got seats on the board.

I shared the news with my mother, who immediately assumed the worst. She hates Amber and has trust issues in general, so the next thing I knew, the lawyers and publicists were involved. They ran scenarios for every possible way Amber and the boys could try to take something away from us or make the business and the family look bad.

Eventually, the lawyers assured us that there was no way to break the will or her non-disclosure agreement, so our assets were safe. However, the publicists cautioned that the boys might claim to have information that could tarnish Grampy's legacy or damage the family's reputation. The boys are not bound to silence through any legal agreements or by the terms of their trust funds, and we were strongly cautioned that they could use this as leverage in any negotiations with the family—because, of course, it was assumed they would be looking to negotiate a better deal with us, just as their mother had done years before.

My mother was incensed by this potential loophole and announced that the discussion with the boys had to be face-to-face. There was some back and forth over whether I should go or Jonny, who was emerging as a talented problem solver. It was decided that I would go, since the boys reached out to me and it might antagonize Amber if we sent Jonny instead, so I was dispatched to London and my mission was to check out the boys and to see if I could uncover what they and their mother really wanted from us. I was to be cordial but non-committal if they revealed their demands. I was being sent on a reconnaissance mission only—I was not authorized to negotiate with them.

Amber answered the door herself and greeted me with a hug as she ushered me in from the raw drizzly weather. She was still stunning with the help of some artful fillers along the cheekbones and a very good eyelift—just enough work to keep her beautiful and obscure her age. She was casually elegant in jeans, a gorgeous sky-blue cashmere sweater, and stocking feet.

We walked through the spacious townhouse to find the boys in a cozy wood-paneled room holding back a pair of yellow Labradors that seemed very large and very eager to greet me. As you would expect in London, we had tea with biscuits (shortbread cookies) while we chatted about my trip, and I heard all about the dogs and school. It was a relaxed atmosphere and they were easy to be around. We laughed naturally over the small talk, and the cookies were delicious. Turns out Amber and the boys baked them for me themselves.

Amber excused herself to take the dogs to the park so the boys and I could speak privately. I came prepared to explain the mechanics of the foundation. I'd tell them how many meetings we hold every year, our areas of focus and about the staff—minutiae that would seem helpful but was safe territory.

Before I could start my prepared commentary, Chance earnestly told me he was planning on studying medicine. He'd watched Amber's dad fade away during a battle against Parkinson's disease. His grandfather refused to leave West Virginia, where there were few specialists, which made it difficult to get him the care he needed. As a board member, Chance wanted to see the foundation expand to assist people who didn't have convenient access to medical specialists, maybe through funding for telemedicine services or the creation of a domestic Doctors Without Borders volunteer program. He thought this would fit in nicely with the foundation's mission. It turns out the boys spent several summers in West Virginia with Amber's family, and these vacations left a lasting impression on them. There was something very familiar in the timbre of Chance's voice and in his mannerisms, but I couldn't put my finger on it. As he gestured with a decisive hand chop through the air to make a point, it struck me: of Grampy's five children, Chance is the one who most physically resembles him.

  Thorne wasn't as certain of his path. He was headed to the University of Edinburgh after a gap year teaching English to refugees. His passion was American History. He'd probably have found a better program in the US, but his summers in West Virginia taught him that he simply didn't like living there. Everyone has a comment to make about Grampy, but in London people don't usually put it together that he is one of Grampy's sons. He does look more like his mother, too. Thorne didn't have any thoughts about the foundation other than supporting his brother's idea wholeheartedly. He was clearly the shy one.

When Amber and the dogs returned, we said our goodbyes and then my driver took me to my business dinner in Marylebone. I knew within minutes of taking my seat in the trendy restaurant that we wouldn't be supporting this insignificant little charity whose president was seated across from me. The frumpy man was passionately describing the organization he led as I nodded and occasionally ate a bite of perfectly roasted chicken. It was a waste of time, but I was grateful for the unproductive dinner. It had provided me with a solid reason to limit my time with Amber and the boys and, more importantly, to avoid taking my mother's calls without first having time to reflect on my visit.

When I got back to my hotel room, I fretted over what to tell the family. My mother had already left three voice messages and several texts, so I knew I had better call her soon or she'd send someone over from the London staff to ensure I spoke with her. My topline was that they were really nice young men, but I hadn't asked any probing questions. In fact, I realized I had taken everything at face value. My always-skeptical family, their eager-to-bill lawyers, and the paranoid publicists would be poised to grill me as soon as they could. They would scoff at any declaration that the boys are "nice and sincere" and demand some kind of verification.

They would think I was played. Was I? All my life I'd been taught that Amber couldn't be trusted. Maybe the whole scene was an orchestrated and well-rehearsed performance. That is what we would've done. We only let others see what we want them to see. That's what we would do when the boys joined us for their first foundation board meeting in May. My mother would probably sigh with disappointment, saying that she should've sent Jonny after all. I wouldn't mention the home-baked cookies; that would definitely make my mother think they were playing me.

As planned, the boys arrived in New York in mid-May during an extended streak of picture-perfect weather. We wined them and dined them relentlessly for four days. I took them on a private after-hours museum tour of a sold-out exhibit of contemporary Native American artists, and Chad personally flew them around Manhattan in his helicopter. My mother had a dinner party at her massive brownstone and the guest list included a famous historical documentarian, the dean of the US History department at

Columbia, the lead researcher on Parkinson's disease at Johns Hopkins University, and the governors of West Virginia and New York.

The board meeting went well. We approved the proposed grants and everyone in the family got a little something for their pet cause or to smooth the waters with an industry or country that was giving the family trouble. We didn't discuss this in front of the boys or at the board meeting; those things had been worked out at family dinners, one-on-one breakfasts, or video calls beforehand. What the boys heard were comments endorsing generosity, expressions of gratitude, and my speech about feeling blessed. The boys asked good questions, took notes, and seemed very engaged. The research grant to look at marine animal health in shipping lanes was of particular interest to Chance.

My mother's strategy was to woo them and make them see that being part of the family was better than any challenge to the family that they or their mother were plotting. Once they fell in line, she'd find a little something in or aligned to the business that would keep them close—but not too close.

So, when Amber called and said the boys were going to defer on their board seats, at least until after they finished university, I was dumbstruck. This was not the expected outcome of our carefully strategized, well-rehearsed, and perfectly executed hospitality.

I cancelled my ten o'clock call and sat in my office, staring out the window. I could feel the anxiety rise inside of me as I thought about calling my mother to deliver the news. She would be enraged, seeing this as my fault and another failure. She'd see the boys as an unchecked risk that can come at us and hurt us at any time. She'd scold me and ask me how I let this happen. I didn't have a good answer for her.

While we were patting ourselves on the back for undoubtedly wowing them, had those two nice boys seen through us and in fact been horrified by the self-serving nature of our philanthropy? By our nonchalant excesses? Had they understood they were witnessing a performance? Did they feel manipulated? Did they see that marine research grant as the greenwashing speaking point it was intended to be? Had we underestimated them? I felt myself tearing up with a sense of inexplicable loss combined with a heavy dread.

I knew the answers to my questions: of course they saw through all of it. There wasn't an honest or sincere moment during their entire four days with us. In London, they told me they were looking forward to visiting with the family when they attended the board meeting. I had deliberately ignored that simple and sincere request because I knew it would set my mother off on a furious tangent about Amber. My mother, their sister, had spent no time alone with them. My uncles, their brothers, talked to them about safe and impersonal topics like the cars they owned, the weather, and golf. The boys don't play golf and, like most eighteen-year-old boys, they weren't very interested in barometric pressure. I don't recall anyone asking them if the schedule we arranged interested them or if they had any requests for things to do or see in New York. But, looking back on it, I do remember several long pauses in their conversations with us. Maybe even some side eye now and then.

Then anger welled up inside of me. It made me want to just scream as loud as I could, at everyone. My parents—especially my controlling mother who raised me, as she was raised by Grampy, to distrust almost everyone and to hide my true self at all times. My father, who lived in his imaginary world and avoided the family most of the time. My brother Chad, who worked so hard to be just like our mother and gleefully lauded his status as the heir apparent over me and my cousins. My Yaya, who always pretended not to see the bad stuff in our family and, by turning a blind eye, let it all happen. My cousin Athena, prettier and smarter than I was, always nipping at my heels, leaving me feeling hunted and exhausted daily. But mostly I was angry at Grampy, who ruined all of us with his selfishness, his outsized ego, his greed, and his insistence that we follow the sad example he set for us: one that made it clear that the right tone of voice and the right appearance were what mattered. *Actually* doing the right thing was not required. Always guard what belongs to the family. Always know your role in the family and appear to be in character. If you didn't adhere to his rules, if you dared to veer from the plan, he'd freeze you out and cut you down with his poisonous words and cold glare. Now my mother has taken on the job of role model—or enforcer, depending upon your perspective. She's more artful, but she still strikes fear in the hearts of those family members who displease her.

  I looked down at my baby bump and felt my increasingly restless daughter shift inside of me. Another rush of anger spread throughout my body. The family already referred to her as my Mini-Me. Good God, that is not what I want for her. In my head, I screamed. *NO. NO. NO. NO.* I don't want her to be like me: worried, anxious, frustrated all the time; never sleeping through the night, never digesting a meal easily, biting my nails to the quick. I glanced in the mirror on the wall beside my desk. On the outside I looked a little tired, but my face showed no emotion. To some, I might even look serene; yet I was screaming inside my head. I'm always screaming inside my head, but I never break character. Never.

    Shouldn't my pregnancy be an act of hope? A hope that I can create a real family, one like Yaya describes when she talks about her childhood? One like I see my uncle, Jonathan, has with his family? Like I saw with Amber and her boys? There must be a way.

    I decided to call Amber. I wouldn't let on that I wanted to escape like she and her boys did—I wasn't sure how much to trust her—but I was sure I could learn from her. My mother always complained that Amber was gone in the blink of eye after Grampy died, and that there was no chance to establish an agreement about how things would work in the post-Grampy world. What was the narrative for his legacy and how would the family protect it? Who would be in charge of his presidential library? Books, interviews, all the media requests; how would that be handled? As it turned out, Amber wanted nothing to do with any of those things—she just wanted to get away and start her new life outside the spotlight.

When I call her, I'll say I'm calling to apologize for being short with her when we spoke earlier, and then I'll cultivate her as a friend. I'll ask her to help me understand what, if anything, I can do to keep her boys informed about the foundation while they are at university. I'll ask her for advice on raising a child in a famous family. I'll flatter her about what a good job she did as a single mother. This will draw her in and give us a couple of reasons to keep talking to each other.

Later this afternoon, I'll call my friend Dale at Princeton. He asked me to do a couple of guest lectures on philanthropy, and that's a good way to start my move toward a life outside the family businesses. I'll show Dale and his colleagues how well I'd fit into that world. I can soften them up with a donation too; they must have some kind of capital campaign underway. A nice, big donation would make it easy to connect to the right people, like trustees and prominent faculty. They can help me make this happen.

Princeton has a beautiful Gothic campus of stone buildings topped by slate roofs and lots of chimneys. There's a wonderful library, too. It looks so beautiful. No, idyllic—that's a better word. My husband can work remotely. We could buy a house nearby, along the banks of the Delaware river. Maybe in New Hope where there are lots of cute shops and restaurants. My daughter would be safe and happy there. I could be safe and happy there.

Amber

The conversation with my friend Shefali this morning made me uncomfortable. My boys sat with us and the topic of arranged marriage came up. Shefali has an arranged marriage, and she and Rahul have been extremely happy together for almost three decades. I also had an arranged marriage, but my story is very different.

I grew up what they used to call dirt poor in a trailer park with my mother, her sister (Aunt Cissy), and my cousin Evie. My father lived nearby with a series of wives and girlfriends. It surprises most people, but we all got along very well. I don't have stories of physical or substance abuse to confess. My father was actively involved in my life and most of the wives and girlfriends were nice to me. That said, poverty is hard. We were always only one minor emergency away from disaster. Car repairs could mean living on bean soup for weeks. A medical emergency could mean losing the trailer.

All my life, everyone complimented me on how pretty I was—even strangers. So, when I had the opportunity, I went to New York City to become a professional model. I was sixteen and, other than a day trip to Charleston to participate in a modeling competition, I'd never been to a city and I'd never been out of West Virginia. Momma had been on her own since she was fifteen, so she didn't think I was too young to make my own way in the world. Neither of my parents cared much about education, and I think it was always assumed that my beauty was my greatest asset and that was how I would get through life. So Daddy drove me to the train station in Washington, DC, and off I went.

Someone from church found a room for me at a minister's home in Rego Park, Queens. It sounded so glamorous: *Queens*. At least in those days, Queens wasn't glamorous. Additionally, it was a terrifying subway ride into Manhattan, which *was* glamorous even if it was overwhelming. I cried, prayed with the minister and his family, then cried some more.

A few weeks later, the miracle happened, just as we prayed. I was signed by a modeling agency, which moved me to a group apartment with other girls a little older than me, and I started to get modeling jobs. I worked steadily and made good money. I modeled swimwear and back-to-school clothes for ads. I did prom and wedding photo shoots. I did teen magazine fashion spreads and some teen makeup ads. I got invited to events to just "decorate the room." I could finally buy new clothes of my own. Beautiful clothes. Lots of clothes.

Men propositioned me, but I was too scared to date for the first year or so and my agent, Betty, protected me. Then I met David. He had an irresistible British accent and was an investment banker. I had no idea what that was, but he was clearly rich and he lived a life surrounded by beautiful things and he went to beautiful places where I could wear all my beautiful clothes. Before long, I moved into his loft and thought I had found my happily ever after. I even strolled through jewelry stores along Fifth Avenue to look at potential engagement rings. I was eighteen.

David was controlling and emotionally abusive. He liked to tell me about the other beautiful women he'd been with and brag about women who were currently propositioning him. I was constantly worried I would lose him. Then one day he sent my things to a hotel, paid the hotel bill for the next two weeks, called me stupid, and told me we were done. The agency helped me pull myself back together, but they let me know that my work was suffering and I needed to do better immediately or they would drop me. I was twenty-one.

When I aged out of the teen magazines and wedding work, I couldn't break through to the next level and attract any interest from the high-fashion magazines or perfume companies, which was where the big money was in those days. For several years, there was plenty of second-tier advertising work. There were lots of digital catalogues and some ads where I was a young mother buying diapers, cleaning products, or pet food. Then the work began to slow down. My look was no longer in high demand, and my career had peaked.

Betty took me to lunch and told me it was time to think about the next stage of my life. I had no education, no special talents, and no vision for my future. She advised me to marry well.

Betty made sure I was invited to the kinds of events where I could meet an appropriate husband. One day, she showed me a group photograph from a recent fundraiser. I was standing next to a portly older man I vaguely remembered meeting. It seems I made a good impression on him and he wanted to take me to dinner. Betty was adamant: don't sleep with him—not yet. We went to dinner a few times and I firmly but diplomatically rejected his advances. He didn't push too hard, unlike most of my other dates.

Soon Betty had good news: he needed a pretty wife for companionship and to help him entertain. He'd been married before and wasn't looking for the love of his life. He thought I had potential. We were now going to "go official" as a couple and raise our profile. This meant attending galas, the theater, golf tournaments, and other events where we would be seen together. I worked with his staff to know what was expected of me and they took over handling the logistical side of my life. I signed a non-disclosure agreement that Betty assured me was a standard practice with wealthy, well-known people. I had a clothing allowance and I had a car and driver available for all my appointments. I received flowers every Monday morning. He started to pay my rent. He gave me a big diamond bracelet. My life was very busy and pretty cushy.

Betty informed me that as a couple, we had been well received by the media. He was especially pleased with the *New York Post* page six item headlined "Young Love." She had a meeting with him later that day to see if he was ready to move things along.

I look back on all of this now and wonder how I didn't notice that we never talked about the relationship or anything of substance. Even on our dates, it was always about showing me off and getting a read on how things appeared to others. On the way over, we discussed who we needed to meet and our goals for the evening. On the way home, we assessed our success. Did my dress get compliments? Did we meet the right people? Did they look at us with envy? Were there any follow-up items, like meeting for lunch or even a phone call? He also stopped trying to sleep with me.

Then the negotiations began. Apparently, it was an embarrassment that I hadn't finished high school. A story was constructed that when I came to New York, I got a tutor from a Christian academy and earned my diploma. I agreed to tell that story. I know now that he bought the diploma for me. David was also bought off to ensure he wouldn't come forward and damage our reputation. I agreed to refer to David as my "brief teenage infatuation," if the subject ever came up.

I approved the engagement ring, which looked more like a small satellite dish than a beautiful piece of jewelry. I eagerly accepted my annual clothing and beauty allowances. I agreed to maintain my weight and get prior approval on changes to my hair from him or his designated staff member. Betty assured me that the language about how often and what kind of sexual relations we would have was just standard stuff in a prenup. The infidelity clauses were also just "boilerplate." When I insisted that I wanted children, the negotiations came to a halt.

Lucky for me, when he went out by himself to dinner and to the theater the paparazzi would shout, "Where's Amber?" and one outlet implied that he couldn't hold on to "the young beauty." It was agreed I could have one complete pregnancy.

And so, we were married. Betty was right about almost everything, though I wish I had slept with him before we announced our engagement. He was a cruel lover who had no interest in my pleasure and, in fact, liked to see me look humiliated or uncomfortable and sometimes laughed when he was done. I think he wanted to make sure I knew I was nothing more than property to him. I like to think I wouldn't have gone through with the marriage if I'd known about this behavior, but in all honesty, I probably would've married him anyway. I knew Betty had arranged the best marriage she could for me and the threat of being poor again gave me the shakes.

The boys think we met at a party and he swept me off my feet with grand romantic gestures that helped me get past the big age difference. I don't think I could ever bring myself to tell them the truth, and I don't see any reason they need to know that I basically sold myself to their father.

When he was elected president, I was in disbelief but prepared to do my bit, just as I had on the campaign trail. I'd stand by his side and look beautiful. I also looked forward to finding a cause I could champion, like all the First Ladies before me. I could do something important and lasting, and the idea both scared and thrilled me. But when his daughter Vivian made it clear that she would be working in his administration and taking on many of the traditional roles of the First Lady, I called Betty.

Betty advised me to stay in Manhattan and refuse to move to the White House until he renegotiated the prenup. She said I had leverage now as it would draw too much negative attention if I didn't join him in Washington. He increased my clothing allowance. He increased the boys' trust fund. He said we could have a dog. But he dug in his heels on Vivian taking the role as the lead woman representing the family in the White House; or, as I saw it, as co-First Lady.

I wanted to hire staff but I was told I'd have to wait until Vivian had fully identified the staff and budget she would need. *She* was asked to oversee and approve *our* living quarters at the White House! I sent him an idea I had for an initiative to help rural schools and was told that was more in Vivian's area of responsibility. She let me know that wasn't something she wanted to focus on and I should just be patient and she'd let me know which projects I'd be assigned. So Betty and I went silent.

Vivian was photographed with a prominent designer rumored to be creating her ball gown for the inauguration. Vivian hired a high-profile woman as her Chief of Protocol. Vivian gave an interview about her vision for the future of American women. This only made the media more curious about my absence. Was I sick? Was I pregnant again? Were we getting a divorce? Where was I? Christmas was a week away and the inauguration was getting very close. The media was becoming obsessed with my absence. He caved, but he never forgave me.

Ours was never a storybook romance, but after we renegotiated everything, he was very cold to me—even hostile behind closed doors. I tried a few times to break through and reestablish a more cordial partnership for the sake of the boys, but he was under siege from all sides almost from the day he took the oath of office. He didn't have the energy for, nor the interest in, working things out with me. I was a little sad for the boys, but overall, I was relieved. He was a terrible man and the less we had to be around him, the better for all of us. He had a foul mouth and a mean streak that made him distrust everyone and criticize everything. He was about the worst role model I can think of for children. Vivian and Jonathan are really screwed up, and Jamie is only okay because Margeaux raised him pretty much on her own in California.

Once I had the boys, I was always thinking about how I could get them away from him and where we would go when I got my chance. So when he died, I knew we were headed for London as soon as possible. I would buy a gleaming white townhouse with a walled garden where the boys could play with their friends and I could sip tea with my friends. I'd put big pots of bright red geraniums by the front door every summer. We'd get a second dog and maybe a cat too. I started packing the night he died.

Sometimes I think about how cool it is that it's my inaugural ball gown that hangs in the Smithsonian Museum and not Vivian's gown. My beautiful peacock blue chiffon gown, with just a little sparkle to catch the light when I walked and he swirled me for our photo op dances. Kids look at it on school trips and families on vacations. It's not the meaningful legacy I wanted when he was elected, but it is something that is lasting and beautiful and has my name on it. Just my name. Not his name. Not Vivian's. Just mine.

"Patience and perseverance, my girl." I can still hear Betty saying that to me in her husky voice as she guided me through the rough patches. It doesn't make how he and his family treated me okay, but my boys were worth half a dozen horrible years with him. And I've got a good life here in London. It's even better than I imagined on all those lonely days and nights in the White House. Betty was right. God bless Betty.

Vivian

I had just returned to my office from a highly contentious meeting about reorganizing the management of our airline when the call came that Daddy had a stroke and was dead. That horror show Amber didn't even call me herself, some assistant delivered the news. Amber was probably too busy doing a dance of joy up and down the halls of our family retreat in Bridgehampton to call me personally. She and Daddy had secluded themselves in the house since the inauguration of his successor after he lost the election. The media declared that Daddy was being surprisingly respectful of the new president by uncharacteristically staying out of the spotlight. I knew from our daily conversations that he was seething with rage, plotting revenge, and obsessing over how best to make his return to the public eye. He wasn't going to let anyone outside the family see him lose his shit—that would be out of character for him—so "sources close to the former president" let key media players know that he was being gracious, statesmanlike, taking the high road, putting the country first, and all that PR crap.

The assistant who called me also requested that I tell my mother before the news broke in the next couple of hours. I knew I had to tell her in person, as she would become hysterical despite the fact that they had been divorced for decades. And she did exactly that, sobbing uncontrollably. I handed her over to Jonathan so I could get to Bridgehampton as quickly as possible. Amber would be in way over her head trying to handle a delicate situation like this, and she could make a huge mess of things if I didn't step in immediately.

I love my mother, but my father was not good at choosing wives for himself. My mother was beautiful, an obedient wife, a dedicated parent, and a great golfer. She learned to set a pretty table and dress elegantly, but she wasn't well-educated and she isn't a deep thinker. If she had understood the world she was living in a bit better, I think she could've held onto my father and spared my brother and I from those step-monsters.

Amber, the last and worst of the step-monsters, had been able to sweeten her prenup when Daddy was elected President. After his death, we learned that he left her the Hamptons estate. We were dumbfounded; this was our family sanctuary, and now it belonged to

Amber. She had complete control over if, when, and how we could visit; she could redecorate, which she was forbidden from doing when Daddy was alive; she could even sell the property to someone else. That was unacceptable, so we made her a fair market offer for it. She moved to London and let it sit empty for two years while we haggled over the price. Two years! Eventually we gave in and paid her millions of dollars too much, but it was ours again. I'll never forgive her.

And now, years after his death, she is trying to reinsert herself into the family. First, she sent her sons for a visit under the guise that they wanted to join the board of our family foundation, but now I'm sure it was some kind of information gathering mission. On top of that, she is befriending my daughter Allegra. It's clearly a carefully thought through strategy, but I still can't figure out her end game. There doesn't seem to be any real gain for her except to get under my skin, but maybe that's enough for that conniving bitch.

Allegra is educated and well-traveled, but I worry that she is an unsophisticated thinker like my mother. Maybe some of it's my fault. She spent too much time with my mother when she was a child, and children absorb everything they experience no matter how hard you work to shape and steer them. I'd bring her to the office and she'd just sit on the floor with a book—usually about something completely inane like butterflies or castles. She'd smile and be polite, but she wouldn't really engage with anyone in the office. She wasn't curious about the business—not one bit. Her head was always in the clouds. So sometimes I'd send her to my mother's for a weekend or even a week because, frankly, she annoyed me.

Now she's about to become a mother herself. Maybe she'll finally develop a more reality-based perspective and stop torturing me with periodic threats to go off and become a professor or a librarian or one of the other fluffy little jobs that she becomes infatuated with for a time. Like my mother, her instinct is to avoid confrontation and hide from anything difficult. It is exasperating.

I'm more like my father's mother, Eileen. I meticulously examine all sides of a thing to avoid unintended consequences. They don't happen on my watch. I am patient, strategic, and carefully pick my spots before I act. I can go toe-to-toe with anyone, and I'm nobody's fool. On my grandmother's tomb, beneath her name, there is one word: *Formidable.* When my time comes, I want them to put

Formidable 2 on my tomb. That used to make Daddy laugh, and he'd say with affection, "You are just like her."

I also have Eileen's perfect profile. I know that sounds shallow, but I don't care. I like that I look like her. I like that I act like her. I feel lucky to have known her before Alzheimer's stole her away from us and all that wisdom vanished. She was strong and smart and ahead of her time in many ways. She was truly extraordinary. I wish Allegra had seen her in action.

I'm still hoping that after running the foundation for a few years she'll finally grow up and my daughter will come over to the business side. I've had glimpses of a real talent for negotiation. When she gets out of her own way, finding a mutually acceptable deal comes naturally to her, but usually she needs to be pushed to look beyond the obvious, to recognize people's true motives and to stand up for the family's best interests.

Her cousin Athena could easily take over the foundation and it's obvious she wants a bigger role. After the baby is born, I think I'll stoke their rivalry a bit to see if I can move things along. If I can get Allegra to see a new role on the business side as an escape from tensions at the foundation, I'm sure I can convince her to make the move.

Daddy would never have tolerated that kind of nonsense about libraries, archives, or a secluded life in academia from Jonathan and me. We always knew that our future was tied to the family business and Daddy's ambitions. "Resistance is futile," we'd chant, mimicking the Borg from *Star Trek*, a favorite childhood TV show of ours. Somehow, we knew that the worst thing we could do was disappoint him. He'd give you a chilling look and then ignore you for days, in some cases weeks. It frightened us. We were sure we would be left behind like our mother and that would be intolerable.

I can see that he was a little harsh at times, but it worked. We never made the same mistakes twice; after a while, we didn't make any mistakes at all. And look at the global enterprise he built for us and we are now running! That type of consistent family leadership and ongoing success doesn't happen on its own. I'm grateful to Daddy for what he taught me.

The rules were simple. Everything is about the family brand. Make people wish they were us, but be sure they aren't jealous. They need to feel we deserve all the good things in our lives. They need to see us as special, not merely lucky. We need to be almost like American royalty: above reproach. The bad, messy stuff is never seen outside the family. If the public doesn't doubt us, they won't doubt the business. In fact, people will want us to succeed. They'll want to believe that we are living out their fantasy lives. They will want to be near us, to work with and for us. To somehow, even in a tiny way, be adjacent to our perfect lives. That game plan worked like a charm until Daddy was elected president.

The first campaign was one of the best experiences of my life. People thought of my father as a hero and they cheered him on. Day after day, tens of thousands of supporters would gather and shout his name, expressing hope and even reverence. I'd look out at a sea of people dressed in shirts and hats with his name. The media courted and flattered him. He charmed the country in his interviews, wowed them with his speeches, decisively won his debates. It was a landslide victory. The fact that it could end four years later with a landslide defeat is still hard to process.

Almost from day one, things went wrong for him. People came out of nowhere with petty grievances that they turned into unflattering books. A cyberattack from terrorists, natural disasters, a shaky economy, a massive salmonella outbreak. He was under siege on all fronts, domestic and foreign. He became ill-tempered, paranoid, and vindictive. He couldn't consistently maintain his "I've got it all under control" demeanor in public. He snapped at everyone with hurtful, biting comments. Sometimes he fired people just because he was having a bad day. His approval numbers plummeted and the rage farmers in the media turned on him.

I'll admit it had been a few years since he was involved with the day-to-day running of the business and his approach to management was both out of date and not as effective as it could've been, but that is why I was there. I lined up a lot of good people for the administration, but when it started to hit the fan, it came fast and furiously and we never caught up. We no sooner brought in the best experts and formed a coalition to address the national security crisis than an earthquake hit. Once we got our heads around rebuilding a major city center and mourning our dead, the salmonella thing happened and more people died. This was followed by a very active hurricane season. The bad news and the bad luck never ended, and before we knew it, the reelection campaign was underway.

The second campaign was a nightmare and, as if the political part wasn't difficult enough, Jonathan's wife Sarah had a late-term miscarriage on the last night of the convention. After that, Jonathan's heart and head weren't in the campaign. In a weak moment during an interview, he shared some family history about Mom and Daddy's divorce and how it affected him. Taking Jonathan's quote out of context, the media ran with "Son says, 'He isn't the man I thought he was.'" Daddy's opponent adopted the slogan *Not the man we thought he was!*

Everything was filtered through that statement until Election Day. The president said he would do this or the president says he will do that but can we believe him? Is he the man we thought he was? We were doomed.

Daddy never forgave Jonathan and never spoke to him again. He told me he was revising his will and he planned to cut Jonathan out of it. He was going to leave him a dollar just to drive home the point. Of course, my brother would still be an extremely wealthy man thanks to trusts and his substantial personal real estate holdings, but he'd be deeply wounded by Daddy disinheriting him. I should've tried to change his mind, but I didn't. I was back in the CEO role for barely two months, so I didn't have a lot of time to mediate family squabbles. Jonathan didn't exactly welcome me back with open arms either, and I'll admit I resented his lack of visible enthusiasm for my return.

He had his shot at the top while I was in DC and he didn't distinguish himself in any way. He just settled for maintaining the status quo. You can't do that in business; you are actually losing ground if you aren't growing your business. Competitors will take advantage of you and before you know it, business starts slipping away. He said I didn't understand how hard it was to run things when Daddy was president. Almost everything was a conflict of interest and it felt like the risk and compliance office was in charge. Pure bullshit.

Jonathan is much better at the tactics than leadership and I think, if he's honest with himself, he's been more content in the operational role he took on after I returned from DC. It gave him plenty of time for Sarah and his kids. They are a tight little unit, always texting and talking to each other throughout the day. Lots of inside jokes. Jonathan and Sarah still hold hands sometimes, too. It's not my style but I know him well enough to see that their affection is genuine and I'm happy for my brother. Though I do find it all a bit Hallmark Channel sappy.

I don't have the luxury of indulging in that sort of thing. I have to be willing to miss some traditional family time for the overall good of the entire family. The wellbeing of the family business is ultimately the wellbeing of the family, and it sits on my shoulders. We all understand that.

That's one of the reasons I'd like Allegra to come over to the business side, so she can see through adult eyes what my life is like and the sacrifices I make. I can feel that she still resents all the regattas and flute recitals that I missed. She says she understood why I missed her high school graduation, but I'm not convinced. If she was here, she'd see how that trip to China was essential to our long-term success and put us out in front of all the other shipping organizations. It is unfortunate that the meeting had to happen the same day she graduated, but it couldn't be helped. And besides, it was years ago.

My future granddaughter needs to see her mother stepping up, too. I'm not going to repeat the mistakes I made with her mother and let her hide in a fantasy world. I'm going to introduce her to the business from day one and make sure she understands her obligations. We can even build a nursery up here next to the executive offices. Hopefully this move will finally motivate Allegra to wholeheartedly embrace her birthright. I have no doubt moving to the business side is the right thing for Allegra, and I know once she makes the move, she'll be happy here.

Gigi

Here's the story of my life:

    I can't believe he loves me.

    I can't believe we're married.

    I can't believe I'm living this life.

    I can't believe he left me.

    I can't believe he's remarried.

    I can't believe he's President.

    I can't believe he's dead.

We met cute in a small college town in the Finger Lakes region of New York at the start of his sophomore year at the local university. In those days it was common for the neighborhood grocery store to stack fresh produce to display it. I bumped into the overly full pile of oranges and they started rolling all over the place. I was chasing them and he jumped in to help me. We laughed and laughed until tears were rolling down our cheeks. At one point, he brushed my hand and I literally felt electricity pass between us. I know that sounds like I imagined it or I am romanticizing the past, but I'm not. That moment was very real. Of course, Vivian thinks it was static electricity. She is just like his mother and doesn't have a romantic bone in her body.

  He started hanging out at my father's pizza shop where I had been waitressing since graduating from high school the previous spring. We went for long walks by the lake and talked for hours. He told me how he felt punished and exiled by his father. He hadn't wanted to leave Manhattan and go to school in the middle of nowhere. He was homesick for New York City and he missed everything about it. He was bored with his business classes. They seemed pointless. After all, he was going to work at the family company and eventually take it over. His family owned parking lots all over New York City. I didn't realize what a lucrative business that was as most of the parking in my town was free in those days.

  I went on the pill and he rented a beautiful cabin on the shore of Lake Skaneateles. It wasn't a tourist destination in those days, so we were sure no one would see us and my parents wouldn't know that I lied about visiting a high school friend who was going to college in Ithaca. We made love at dusk and lay in each other's arms as the moon rose in the sky. It was my first time, and while he claimed to be experienced, I am sure that it was his first time too. He was gentle and sweet. He told me how much he loved me. After that we couldn't keep our hands off each other.

My parents liked him, mainly because he clearly adored me and they had that in common. His parents didn't want to meet me. After eighteen months together, they finally relented and let me come with him to Manhattan for a weekend visit. They were polite but condescending. Shortly after our visit, they insisted he break things off with me for the summer to test our relationship, claiming we were too young to be so serious. His father threatened and bullied him until he agreed to the temporary pause. We both cried when he left. In my mind I can still see him driving off in his boxy little red BMW and remember the gut-wrenching emptiness and fear I felt.

We kept our word to his parents and there were no secret letters or calls. He worked alongside his father half the day and then played golf or tennis at the country club. His mother set him up on a series of dates with the daughters of family friends and clients, but none of them sparked any interest in him. He told me all he had to do was look at the picture of me sitting on a bench next to Lake Skaneateles and he knew who he wanted. It's a funny picture. My hair was almost to my waist in those days, and I usually tied it back in a ponytail or a braid, but on this day, I let it hang loose. It was windy, so in the picture my long, dark curls are swirling about my head. I look wild and free. No one would ever describe me as wild and free, and yet that is probably the best picture anyone has ever taken of me.

    Just before he returned for his senior year, he sent a letter asking me to meet him inside the entrance of the grocery store where we chased the oranges two years before. I'd expected him to embrace me and kiss me and tell me how much he missed me—something dramatic and even cinematic—but he was very serious and in a hoarse voice he told me to come with him. He took my hand and marched me a few feet deeper into the store. His hand was cold and damp. I started to get anxious. I avoided looking at him, afraid of what I would see. This was not the joyful reunion I had fantasized about during that endless summer. I had longed for his touch, his smell, the sound of his voice, even just his proximity. I didn't understand his behavior and I was scared.

He let go of my hand and croaked my name. I looked over at him as he got down on one knee and held an open ring box in his hand. I think he asked me to marry him, but by that point the adrenaline was cursing through my body and I was hyperventilating. I could no longer comprehend what was happening. Tears were rolling down my face and I was shaking. He stood up, took me in his arms, and repeated the question. "Yes," I whispered. He announced to the crowd, "She said yes!" and they broke into applause and cheered. My parents and my brother Nick rushed to us from one of the aisles where they were hiding and we all hugged and laughed in front of a stack of oranges.

By today's standards, it wasn't a big ring, but it was the most beautiful thing I had ever seen. And it was from Tiffany's, which in my mind was the ultimate in jewelry and class. A perfect, simple round solitaire on a bright gold band. I still have it and sometimes I put it on at night and go to sleep wearing it.

I signed paperwork describing what I'd receive if we divorced or he died suddenly. My father and mother read it and we thought it seemed fine—after all, this was a forever marriage, so it was just something to calm down his unhappy parents. At the time, my parents were primarily focused on how sad they were that I was moving to New York City and that their future grandchildren would live so far away.

The wedding was the Saturday after his graduation. It was emotional and intimate and then we spent two glorious weeks in Bermuda where he taught me to play golf. Turns out I'm a natural. Also turns out, golf kept me sane in the dark days.

Those first years of marriage were almost perfect. We went to his parents' house in Water Mill in the summer and to his parents' house in Old Naples in the winter. We played lots of golf at our private clubs. He worked reasonable hours and we still took long walks together, but now they were along the East River or by the sea. Under his mother's guidance, I learned how to dress and how to decorate and how to entertain. I was eager to learn and eager to please, and I'm very observant, so it wasn't difficult to figure it all out. Besides, I'm an excellent cook and people loved to come to our place for dinner.

Shortly before our second anniversary, we started our family. First Vivian, and then Jonathan. We were a snuggly family. We snuggled with the kids at night and they jumped into our bed to wake us in the morning. I had housekeepers and a nanny, so things ran smoothly and we still had lots of time together.

His family was cool to me, and at times even mean, but they adored the kids. His father was getting older and started to put pressure on him to be more serious about the business. His father bought a smallish shipping business and gave it to him to run. It came with a warning that he had to make it a success or risk losing his spot as the heir apparent. There was an ambitious cousin with a freshly minted MBA eagerly waiting for his chance to jump the line.

Immediately, our lives changed. He worked every day and he worked long hours. His father and mother monopolized his time. The shipping company thrived, so they bought other small businesses and eventually larger companies. No time for snuggling and long walks now. He was short with the kids. His administrative assistant bought my birthday and anniversary presents. We had our own much grander ocean front place in Bridgehampton and a Mediterranean-style villa in an exclusive golf community in Naples. He'd join us when he could, but at least half the time he had to cancel on us. We celebrated our fifteenth anniversary two weeks late because he couldn't come back from Sidney in time. Some deal was at a critical stage. He was exhausted but refused to take a break from work. The media took notice of his success and he was widely acclaimed for the global empire he had built from what they described as the "simple family business." His parents beamed with pride.

Much of the time in those final years together, I didn't know where he was and he rarely asked me about my life. I tried to arrange family time and activities he'd enjoy, but nothing the kids and I did was good enough. I wanted to protect them from his stinging criticisms, so I started to carve out a separate life for the kids and myself. I cried myself to sleep a lot.

When his father was diagnosed with stomach cancer, it came as a tremendous shock. They gave him only ninety days to live and his father didn't even make it that long. By now, his role as successor was secure and his father told him that it gave him great peace of mind to know he would step into the role of CEO. He'd be completely at peace, except for one thing: if only his son had a wife that was worthy of him, a true partner, someone who was more of an asset to the family, like his mother. Then he'd know everything was going to be fine. His father was such a manipulative snake.

He didn't divorce me immediately, but his father's words ate away at him and we were living separate lives anyway. I'm guessing his father had been planting little negative seeds about me during our entire marriage. He never missed a chance to get in a dig at me when the family was together, so I assume he knocked me behind my back too.

His mother wasn't much better, and after his father passed, he spent more time with her than with me. She never missed an opportunity to mention my lack of a college education or to point out some all-American blonde beauty I should "try harder to be like". Her tone and her expression made it clear she thought I was a hopeless case, and he could and should do better. Then one day, a lawyer came by and explained it all to me. Twenty years, two teenage children, and it was over. My friends told me to fight for myself, as my settlement was going to be very modest. I sent him a dozen oranges. He threw in the Naples house.

I can't believe I spent my life loving that man.

Margeaux

When I was younger, my thing was playing the stereotypical dumb blonde who really isn't dumb at all. I was *never* dumb, but I was hell-bent on getting out of Fresno, I had the right look for those kinds of parts, and I knew how to leverage it. An ad campaign for a chain of ice cream stands in Northern California and a tight tank top were my ticket to LA, and then on to New York City. I can still rock a tank top.

      For almost fifteen years now, I've been playing the signature character for an insurance company's ad campaign. I love the character because she morphed from that always underestimated dumb blonde to a respected, savvy expert people seek out for advice. She's smart and witty and beloved. I get to use my improv and comedic skills too. The insurance company sells dolls, T-shirts, and lots of other merch based on my character on their website, and I get a percentage. It's a dream job. I'd like to think I won the role because of my talent, but I know that my notoriety as his ex-wife was why they initially cast me, and that's fine with me. I've proven my value ten times over.

I met him at a big lawn party in the Hamptons. It wasn't love at first sight—in fact it was never about love—we just got each other. He was tired of dating. I was tired of dating. He didn't want someone who was needy. I wanted to keep working and maintain my independence, but I also wanted some security. I didn't mind being arm candy, especially in his social circle where money was no object and everything was first class. He needed arm candy who was a decent conversationalist, an able hostess, and looked great in a photo. Sign me up! I mean, why not? Neither one of us thought it would last forever, but it suited us at the time.

We had our routines: summer in the Hamptons, galas and fundraisers in the spring and fall, dinner and sex twice a week, and we threw an over-the-top holiday party in December. His kids were grown but they still came to the Hamptons for the month of July and spent many weekends with us. I got some small speaking parts in two films and several guest spots on network TV shows. I had a key supporting role in a limited-run off-Broadway play—and decent reviews, too. Then I got pregnant. We were both surprised. Motherhood wasn't a priority for me and I was very careful with my birth control.

When Jamieson was born, he insisted on a paternity test, which really pissed me off. When he was 100 percent sure Jamie was his son, we settled back into our routine. The only difference was that I was besotted with my son. I couldn't get enough of him. I thought he was the most perfect being on earth. He didn't spend much time with Jamie, but I didn't care because I could make all the decisions about Jamie's life without interference.

Shortly after Jamie turned two, we attended the Academy Awards, when they were still a big thing. At an after-party, he met a producer who pitched him an idea for a reality TV show called *Ruthless*. The producer wanted him to host the show. We both thought the idea was insane. He was a businessman, not a game show host. But the producer persisted. From my vantage point, it looked almost like a courtship with a steady stream of calls, notes, dinners, gifts, and flattery. In fact, I think they even sent flowers a couple of times.

I knew he was bored with the day-to-day of the business. By then it ran like a Swiss clock and was obscenely profitable. He now had a small army of presidents and senior VPs of this and that who ran the airline, the container ship business, the overnight delivery company, and an assortment of other things in his vast transportation empire. And, as she had been groomed to do all her life, Vivian was by his side overseeing everything. She is a brilliant businesswoman and an outstanding leader, wise well beyond her years. More and more, he deferred to Vivian and let her take the lead, so I wasn't completely surprised when he agreed to make the pilot. He's the kind of man that periodically needs to change things up.

When the pilot was picked up, we rented a house in Pacific Palisades so we could easily commute back and forth with Jamie while he was filming. I was thrilled to be back home in California even part-time, and he loved the entire television experience. Who wouldn't? They treated him like a king. He was flattered and pampered in a way that didn't happen in the business world. Sure, sucking up to the boss happens, but it's usually more subtle. More like, "That's another great idea, sir."

On the set of the show, it felt like everyone was devoted to making him not just comfortable but happy—very, very happy. Did he need some water? A salad? A cup of tea from leaves grown in the Himalayas that were handpicked by elves? Did he want to meet this star or that one? Did he need a foot massage? Did he want to drive around in a vintage Aston Martin or a yellow Ferrari? Of course, he could buy or have someone arrange all of this for him anyway, but the assistants and executives at his company didn't sit around all day thinking of big and small ways to make him happy. In La La Land, they did. In fact, for some people on the set, that was literally their full-time job. It's very seductive, especially for someone like him who needs to be the center of everyone's attention.

The show was an instant hit. You never can tell in the entertainment business. He may be a paunchy older man with average looks and a mean temperament in person, but on camera he came across as worldly, visionary, and a sophisticate who didn't suffer fools easily. He would toss out an amusing story about a dinner in Rio or a successful deal in South Korea and bring a new level of energy to an otherwise dry competition about managing a business. One review called him the James Bond of the business world.

No, really. Someone actually wrote that in a review.

When the second season ended, a book was published that he supposedly authored and he went on a speaking tour. We didn't see him for weeks, and he rarely called home. Now, instead of corporate executives at his beck and call, he had publicists, schedulers, personal assistants, and an agent attending to him. He was living in a new world and I wasn't invited to be part of it.

Even though I knew going into the marriage that we wouldn't last forever, I was still sad when it came to an end. I missed our routine. When he told me that he would be filing divorce papers, I accepted it and we parted amicably. The prenup clearly detailed what I would get and while the media portrayed it as "stingy" and "cheap" I was satisfied, especially since Jamie was well taken care of with a sizeable trust fund and living allowance. He also bought us a sweet house of our own in Pacific Palisades. Jamie and I had a wonderful time living in that house. I even married my husband Tony in the backyard by the pool.

I had lunch with his first wife Gigi after the divorce. She wanted to be sure Jamie and I were okay. She is a lovely person. At one point, she told me that as he aged, he became more like his father and I could tell this troubled her deeply. I never knew his father so I couldn't say, but I can say he has a lot of anger toward his dad. He has a lot of anger in general. It's made him mean and cold and not a great parent. I also think he should never have divorced

Gigi. He would've been a lot happier, but it worked out pretty well for me.

Suzy

I met him when his airline's ad agency was developing a new marketing campaign. I was one of four redheaded flight attendants selected to do test shots with him, the new owner of my employer Red Tail Air. RTA was a regional airline founded by two retired fighter pilots. Our longtime logo was a soaring Red-tailed Hawk and our major selling point was serving freshly baked chocolate chip cookies to the passengers, but the new owner and his new agency were going to take us in a very different direction. Their campaign would have lots of double entendres about tails and red-hot good times. I wasn't chosen to do the ads, but I caught his eye and he asked me out to dinner.

    In those days I liked to party—a lot. He was freshly divorced from his first wife and trying to live up to the tabloid coverage that portrayed him as a ladies' man. We were both out to have a good time and neither of us was looking for a long-term commitment. He took me to the best restaurants and booked us into luxurious suites at five-star hotels. He didn't take me to any of his business or society events, and I knew I wasn't going to meet the family. That was fine with me. I didn't want to be accountable to anyone —especially a husband. I've always been fiercely independent.

Most nights when we met at a hotel, he ordered pizza and beer. He had a thing for Greek pizza. I got the lobster or a steak and a nice bottle of champagne from the room service menu. I could order anything I wanted, so I did.

Sometimes he asked me do a little role playing. I was always game. I might be his teacher and make him do extra credit work so he wouldn't fail, or I'd wear my uniform and provide full service for my favorite passenger. Once I was a nurse and we literally played doctor. He never stayed the night.

Because he enjoyed beer so much, I suggested that he go to Germany for Oktoberfest. He loved the idea, and I was surprised when he asked me to go with him. We had a ball until the last night. We were very drunk, and he held me down and made me do something sexually that I didn't like at all and it hurt me. Physically.

I was clearly very upset, so he said it was my turn to be in charge. I could pick anywhere in the world to visit and he'd make it happen. I picked Las Vegas. I knew he didn't like Las Vegas—he thought it was sad and seedy—but I wanted to make him do something he didn't like.

    A couple of weeks later we flew to Vegas. He got us great seats for the show I wanted to see and he made reservations at the restaurants where I wanted to eat. We gambled a little. I like craps. He tried blackjack. Neither of us won more than fifty bucks. Mainly we drank. We drank all day and we drank all night. Somewhere along the line, he switched from beer to Scotch. I think that may be what did him in.

    That night, after we stumbled back into our garishly decorated suite, he sat down on the hideous red velour sofa, put his head in his hands, and started to cry. Then he started to shout. Then more tears. He talked about loneliness and failure. He talked about missing his kids. He hated his father. He cursed him. He hated his mother too. He thought his kids probably hated him. He wanted a dog. He wanted a hug. He said he couldn't remember the last time he was genuinely happy. He was having some kind of breakdown. I didn't know what to do, so I kept pouring drinks. I think I was hoping he'd just pass out.

I'm not sure exactly how it happened—I was blackout drunk—but we got married. I never wanted a husband and children, so I honestly have no idea why I said yes, but I did. I can't imagine how anyone agreed to perform the ceremony—we were certainly both slurring our words and struggling to stand up. But there was paperwork and a very unflattering photo to prove that it happened.

When I woke up the next day, I heard him talking on the phone in the living room of the suite. He was highly agitated and making no effort to keep me from hearing his side of the conversation. I learned later that he was talking to his lawyer. He told him that he had done something really stupid and married this "cheap piece of ass" in Vegas when he was drunk. He was already getting bored with her so he doesn't know what came over him, but somehow she had dragged him to a wedding chapel. That will teach him to go slumming with low rent pussy, he said, sounding very disgusted with himself—and me, too. He ordered the lawyer to fix this mistake and keep it from getting out. The publicity would be disastrous for the company. He'd look irresponsible and out of control. "Make it go away. Fast!" he shouted into the phone.

I wrapped myself in a hotel robe and leaned against the doorway while he finished his conversation. Standing was difficult, but I wanted him to see me. When he turned around and saw me, he flew into a rage. He called me names and accused me of tricking him and getting him drunk deliberately. He said I better not be pregnant because I'd just have to get rid of it. He said a lot of ugly things like that, and even uglier things about me.

I threw up in a wastepaper basket and told him I didn't want to be married to him either. Then I cleaned myself up, got dressed, and went to the airport. I left behind the new clothes and lingerie he bought me for the trip, including the silver sequined cocktail dress that was now ripped and laying on the floor. My wedding dress.

By the time I landed in New York, they had already drafted all the paperwork and his legal representative was waiting outside my apartment building. I didn't ask for anything and I sincerely didn't want anything from him. I just wanted it to be over. He insisted on giving me a generous check and I eventually took it. I read and signed everything. I didn't consult with a lawyer or even a friend. I didn't want anyone to know what had happened. No one. Ever.

I was surprised at how shaky I was following the annulment. I hadn't loved him and I didn't miss him but I couldn't get my bearings. I stopped drinking and using recreational drugs and I started running marathons. I flew for another year or so and then I quit. I didn't fit into that life anymore. Using the settlement money he gave me, I started a travel agency. I specialize in packages for marathoners and extreme sports competitions. I'm not rich but I'm my own boss and I come and go as I please.

When he ran for president, I started to have panic attacks. I didn't want our story to come out. It's sordid. Thinking about it still makes me feel queasy. I couldn't sleep, no matter how many miles I ran that day.

His lawyer called and asked to meet with me. I'd moved out of the city years ago, so the lawyer made the drive to Connecticut and we met on the patio of my little Cape Cod-style cottage. We reassured each other that neither party wanted the story to come out. He offered me more money, but I was afraid that would make it more likely that the story would come out. You know what they say, "follow the money." Instead, I asked him to make a sizeable anonymous donation to a rape crisis center where I volunteer between trips. I signed a new, very stringent non-disclosure agreement and so did he.

Reporters and biographers have reached out over the years, but I never take their calls or the money they offer me. One even became a marathoner and booked a trip through me in the hope of striking up a friendship and finding out what happened between us. It's easy to turn them down and turn them away when you don't want to tell your story.

And for the record, I voted for the other guys.

Sarah

He was an asshole. A total asshole. It had to be all about him, all the time. And I mean *all* the time. I can't remember a family conversation since I met him that wasn't focused on him. He'd trample all over you if you let him, if he could, or if he was just in the mood.

When our baby died, not only did he not call, but he got mad at us. I almost died! The baby *did* die! Jonathan was broken. WTF!

The country and his political buddies all publicly mourned with him. With *him*? The media was faux sympathetic for twenty-four hours. Everyone sent prayers and was keeping him in their thoughts. HIM!

We were the ones in the hospital with baby Amanda, never to breathe a single breath. Away from home. With strange doctors in a strange city. Terrified. Shocked. Grieving. But the world sent their prayers to *him* so he could be strong and stay the course. WTF!

When we left the hospital, someone from the hideous media shouted out at Jonathan and me, "How do you think this will affect the campaign?" What is the matter with people?

Vivian at least called to say she couldn't be with us because there was so much to do with the campaign, and then she checked in regularly to see how we were doing. Gigi, of course, flew in and was there throughout the ordeal, taking care of Jonny and Athena. Even Amber called to check on us and offer any help we needed. She offered to give blood because she's an O negative blood type, a universal donor, but he whisked her out of town before she could get to the hospital. It was more important to him that she stand dutifully and beautifully by his side at a rally than potentially save my life. Margeaux and Jamie sent flowers and a kind note. The flowers were there, waiting for us when we arrived home without our daughter.

Amanda's death wasn't about him, so he never personally acknowledged that his grandchild was stillborn and I spent two days in intensive care. He never called his son to see how he was doing. Never. I'm sure Vivian kept him informed, but that's not the same thing.

His staff sent some kind of communications officer to tell Jonathan to meet with the media outside the hospital and read some statement they wrote about the death of our baby and the status of my health. He was supposed to say he was tired but holding up and that he asked his father to keep campaigning because it was so important to the country. Then he was supposed to sing his father's praises and tell everyone how he was the best candidate and some other bullshit. Again, WTF.

Jonathan refused to leave my side or read the statement. Jonathan is a good man.

I never read the statement Jonathan was supposed to make. I was in and out of consciousness at the time. He told me about it later when I saw the statement the campaign issued without our approval but on our behalf. It was basically the same self-serving crap they wanted Jonathan to spew to the press.

Of course, Jonathan's father didn't miss a beat in his campaign. He never missed Amanda's presence in his life either. I will always miss her.

I often wonder how he would have defended his abominable behavior but I never got a chance to confront him. He cut us off. Cold. He wouldn't take Jonathan's calls, texts, or emails. He wouldn't even let him onto the Bridgehampton property. Once my husband brought the kids out for a visit, and he had the Secret Service make him wait in the car, on the public street with an agent standing guard. So cruel and so humiliating to do that to Jonathan in front of our kids. But I assume that was the point.

It wounded my husband—it was his childhood fear of being cast off by his father come to pass—but I was relieved that we didn't have to be around him anymore. I don't think I could've been civil to him. I think I could've even slapped him. Maybe I'd have thrown something at him. I've imagined doing it. He was a terrible person. I don't miss him.

Athena

I finished looking at the analytics from my publicists and sent a message saying I thought the coverage and posts from yesterday were good. The *Daily Mail Online* was especially amusing with its headline "Leg's Be Charitable" and a photo of me in a red Valentino gown with a slit up to my hip. The caption was good too: who designed the dress, the name of the charity holding the event, and a compliment for my "toned legs." I know it's a trashy rag, but it is always fun and they love me. I also did a short interview with the *South China Morning Post* that appeared yesterday and turned out surprisingly well. It was mainly fashion questions, but then they asked me a couple of serious ones. I nailed them! I toed the family line, but then I shared an appropriate personal experience and showed that I was more than the mere socialite and nepo baby of my official public persona. The headline read: "There's More to Athena Than You Know" with a subhead that said: "A deep thinker with a kind heart." Like I said, nailed it!

My IG remains reliably strong and the reels are doing really well. Later today we'll make another one. I'll be walking my dogs by the river. I'll wear a T-shirt supporting a charity that has an alliance with our airline. I know it will be a tightly fitted T-shirt, because the publicists debated this ad nauseam on our call yesterday. They all had opinions on how tight the T-shirt should or could be. One of them suggested we cut it or tie it to show off my abs. Apparently, the numbers jump whenever I show skin. They collect data on this to help them optimize my media presence.

I'm always amazed that people all over the world will take time to look at me do anything. Literally anything. Last year one of the top performing posts was a photo of me sitting on a bench and staring at the sky. I'm simply staring into space and the photo was liked by thousands of people? In the comments they debated whether I looked like I had the weight of the world on my shoulders, like I was daydreaming about a new man, or even praying. Actually, I was hungry. The ankle boots I was wearing sold out in forty-eight hours, and the designer sent me a pair in every other color to thank me.

All this self-promotion can be tiresome, but it's my job. Give the family a little glamor. Be the embodiment of our enviable lifestyle. Be beautiful. Be beautifully dressed. Be seen in the right places with the right people, and make sure all of it is photographed and publicized. My title is Chief Communications Officer for the family foundation, but I rarely get to do any real work. Between the fittings, fundraisers, public appearances, and photos, there isn't much time for the philanthropy. No, right now, that is Allegra's job.

I put my phone down on the table beside the bed and sink back down into my pile of pillows. The trainer could wait a few minutes this morning. Today would've been Grampy's birthday, and it makes me sad that I didn't have more time with him. I wouldn't be languishing at the foundation if he was still around. I'd be leading it, or at least I'd be leading something in our vast family empire. He wouldn't have let Aunt Viv push me aside.

I may be the only one in the family who genuinely missed him when he died. I was little when it happened, but I loved him very much.

I would sit in his lap and he'd read to me when I visited him at the White House. He read me the Junie B. Jones books. There is a picture of me in his lap in the Oval Office that I have framed on my dresser.

I would call him a couple of times a week just to tell him a joke, too. If he was busy, he'd call me back as soon as he could. I remember his favorite joke was "Why is six afraid of seven? Because seven eight (ate) nine!" He'd laugh every time, as if it was the first time he'd heard the joke.

Grampy loved to laugh, but he didn't do it very often. Even as a young child I knew he was very unhappy. I think that's why I felt the need to tell him jokes. I could make him laugh and I knew that was good for him. He needed to laugh more.

My parents hated him, especially my mother, but Grampy and I had a special bond. I know I was his favorite. He whispered that in my ear right before they took the picture that sits on my dresser. He meant it too.

I liked being his favorite. My mom says I'm too competitive. I *am* very competitive—about everything. I always have been, especially with my cousin Allie. She's Allegra to the outside world, but I've called her Allie since I could talk. I love her like a sister—after all, she's only eight months older than I am. We went to the same schools and the same summer camps. But like sisters, we also have a kind of rivalry. Who ran the fastest? Who was the better poker player? Which of us would be in the first boat on the crew team? Who could win the heart of the captain of the lacrosse team?

Who'd get married first? Allie won that contest. And yes, I admit I am jealous. Plenty of handsome companions, but no true love like my parents or Allie. And that just puts the pressure on me to make sure the wait for Mr. Right pays off with a Mr. Really Amazing.

Allie's insecure about almost everything, but especially her beauty compared to mine. I am more exotic looking; it's a dark, dramatic beauty that photographs well. I get that from Yaya. Allie is more of the all-American country club beauty, like her mother. A little generic, but beautiful just the same.

Allie is also a bit of an intellectual. She reads everything and likes to contemplate human nature and moral dilemmas. I think it's admirable, but I don't really see how it's useful in our world. Maybe she gets this intellectualism from her father, but it's hard to say. I'm not sure I've heard my uncle say much over the years, though I know my father has a lot of respect for him. Or at least he is awed by his endless patience. My auntie is a high-maintenance spouse.

Our rivalry and all her deep thoughts make Allie tense, but I find our competition energizing. It keeps me on my toes. I like being pushed to do more, or challenged to go farther with something, but Allie gets overwhelmed by the pressure. I see it in her face—she gets this tired look, and I can tell she just wants to curl up with a book and escape from the world. Maybe her mother should finally let her go and try life outside of the spotlight that is always on our family, but Aunt Viv would never do that. Auntie needs to be in charge and in control of everything and everyone connected to the family, and she has decided on a career in the family business for Allie. It's just a matter of time before her mother drags her over there. Everyone can see it except for Allie. I'm working behind the scenes to make sure I take over the foundation when the move inevitably occurs. In fact, I finally convinced Auntie to let me take on most of my cousin's role while she is on family leave. I know the family will be watching me closely and I am determined to show them that I'm more than just its most photogenic member.

Maybe I'll call my cousin and see if I can stop by this afternoon when we finish making that reel. I found a first edition of Camus's *The Stranger* for her. Physical books have a calming influence on Allie and she's been notably more tense lately. I know she's anxious about becoming a mom, and by now she knows I'm going to take over for her while she's out. That will certainly add to her anxiety, especially because her mother is pretty aggravated about

Amber's kids not falling in line and she blamed Allie for that screwup. It probably feels like things are being piled up against her. I feel bad taking advantage of her pregnancy, but when opportunity knocks, you need to answer the door. That's a Grampyism. The book will be a nice peace offering, and I'll get her laughing too. My impression of Aunt Viv always works—especially the frosty side eye she gives any of us if we displease her. Allie's just like Grampy that way. She needs to laugh more.

The End

I said, "No. No visitors. Can't you fucking understand English? How loudly do I have to scream so you understand?" I yelled at my assistant Tatiana and practically pushed her out of the door of my office. She is really getting on my nerves because that dumb bitch doesn't listen. There will be no fucking visitors unless I invite them, and I'm sure as hell not ready to issue any invitations. I've been telling her that for months, yet that fucking moron keeps bringing me requests from ghostwriters who want to help with my autobiography, reporters who want to be the first to interview me after leaving office, and even an architect who has the perfect concept for my library.

I usually know exactly what I want to do and how I'm going to do it. I'm known for my decisiveness, but the pathetic truth is that I'm struggling to figure out what comes next. Whatever it is has got to be big—really big. It has to erase all the negative crap that has happened in the last year. It has to restore my image. And I certainly can't accomplish that if I let the world see me aimless and fumbling around, hidden out here on the edge of the country.

Even though the polls weren't great, I never believed I'd really lose the election—but I did. There was no doubt about it. When the election was called, I was shocked, shaken, and angry. I never fail. But this time I did. I called that asshole who is now president and congratulated him, then I went into the hotel ballroom and I made a short but gracious concession speech. I've watched it a couple of times, and fortunately I look and sound strong, unbowed. I was smiling and waving like everything was fine. I even cracked a joke to relieve the tension in the ballroom. You can't tell that I actually felt like I was walking through fog. I was physically cold, almost shivering, and I couldn't clearly see or hear anything. On the video, I see most of the family lined up behind me, subdued but following my lead with smiles, waves, and nods of agreement when I was speaking, but in the moment I didn't even realize they were on the stage with me. Amber came over and took my hand, and then we walked off the stage together. Vivian must've told her to do it, because it would never dawn on dumb bunny Amber to do that on her own. She's too dense.

Tatiana and even Vivian have been nagging me to invite a few close confidants to come out here so it doesn't look like I'm hiding and to "lift my spirits." Vivian says that after the meetings, my friends could leak to the press how well I am doing. They'd report that I'm happy and considering lots of options for what comes next. But I'm not. I'm blocked mentally and feeling stranded here. Anyone I'd invite to visit would see it. They'd be just as likely to tell people I'm incapable of pulling myself together and making a comeback. They'd conclude that I'm finished for good. I can't have that getting out. No, there is just too much reputational risk if I have visitors right now.

    I feel like I'm spinning out of control, and it's terrifying. It's how I felt when I took Sleazy Suzy to Las Vegas. I must've been desperate to even start seeing that piece of trash. She wasn't that pretty and I didn't really like her, but she was convenient and she was game for almost anything in bed. Still, I've had to carry that horrible secret for decades and worry that someday she'll decide she can make more money selling me out than extorting me. I'd be a laughingstock. Tricked by a cheap whore.

    I've got to find a way to turn all this around, to find my way back. I've got to make people admire me again, like they did before

Jonathan shit all over me. Otherwise, it looks exactly like what he said: I'm not the man people think I am. I can't let that stand.

I could call Gigi and see if she'd come out for a visit. I haven't seen her in person in a long time, maybe five years, but we've talked on the phone. She's always warm and I can tell she still cares about me. She also understands me as well as anyone does, and I could use her counsel and perspective.

She's stepped in and helped me before, even after the divorce. When I bought the airline, I was named The Most Intriguing Person of the Year by a very famous TV host for her year-end special. This was a big get. The host wanted me to talk about my mother's Alzheimer's—it wasn't a well-known disease in those days, so this would be sensational but also viewed as brave and a public service. It was perfect for me. We'd walk through the garden of the secluded house in Connecticut facing Long Island Sound where my mother lived in her final years. The audience would see for themselves how my own mother didn't recognize me as her son, or even as a prominent public figure. The irony would be inescapable. It would be heartbreaking but it would also make me more sympathetic, the PR gurus said.

Vivian bragged to Gigi that Daddy and Grandmom were going to be on the special and Gigi called me. She didn't judge. She didn't preach. She simply helped me understand that my mother liked control and she cared about appearances almost above all else. It might hurt that she doesn't recognize me anymore, it might even enrage me, but do I really think that gives me the right to put her in front of the world in such an undignified manner? Someday, that could be me. Would I be comfortable being on display like that? She said it all with kindness—a kindness my mother never showed her. I slept on it and then made the PR guys change how we'd do the interview. The network and the host were not happy, but I agreed to film at the Bridgehampton house and they got over it. The ratings were great. Everyone wanted to get a peek inside the legendary property.

But Gigi might not want to talk to me. She's probably pissed that I won't speak to Jonathan and I can't let her know I have disinherited him. She'll find out when he gets the letter from the lawyers, but she doesn't need to know yet. He deserves this—and maybe even worse than this—for what he did to me, but Gigi won't see it that way and it will upset her.

I'm just so exhausted. I wish I was one of those people who could nap, but that's not me. Plenty of time to sleep when I fucking die. I'll have them bring me more coffee and then I'll call her. I'm sure I can convince her to come out here, but I need to make it happen before Jonathan gets those papers and I've told the lawyers I want them in his hands by the end of the month. Now that will lift my spirits.

Once I get the Jonathan situation finalized, I can start working on divorcing Amber. She is useless, and that greedy whore insisted on getting this house when we renegotiated her prenup. I can't let that happen. I knew it was wrong when I did it, but she had me by the balls. The house should go to Vivian and stay in the family. I'm sure the lawyers can make that happen for me. I pay those fuckers enough that they should be able to do any damn thing I ask.

Still, I have to be careful. I've underestimated Amber before and regretted it. She meets all of her contractual obligations—well, almost all of them. I haven't slept with her in a couple of years now. Not since the night she told me that she could see I was in over my head as President and that it was eating away at me and I was making everyone around me miserable. She had no right to talk to me like that—no right at all—and she knew it. Interfering with or commenting on my professional life is clearly forbidden in our agreement. She's made sure to stay in her lane since that night. I want that trashy bimbo out of my life, and the sooner, the better. It adds more complexity to my reemergence into the world, but I can work it into the overall narrative. I've done that before. It's not hard. I might even work it to get me some sympathy.

Maybe after Amber goes, Gigi could be my plus one when I've got a social engagement. I'm done with marriage for good so I don't see the point in dating, but eventually I'll need someone to accompany me to public functions. We could have a lot of laughs together and the media would love it. She's still a handsome woman and photographs well. I saw her in some photos after Jonathan's wife had that medical issue at the convention and she looked good—very fit and younger than her years. I think partnering with her would be a smart move for me. This feels like a good start in the right direction. I'll just have to get her over the disinheritance thing when she hears about it, but if she thinks I need her, she won't be able to turn her back on me. She never has. We both know she can't. It's not in her nature.

But it's also not a sure thing. Gigi always coddled Jonathan and even supported his marriage to that insipid Sarah, possibly the most boring woman on earth. A *harpsichordist*—who the hell plays the harpsichord in the twenty-first century? She gives these little recitals—pure vanity events—where everyone has to gush over her performance. I went once and I don't know how I managed to get through it. She kept playing what sounded like the same tinny little song over and over again. It was tortuous. Then—without asking—Jonathan bought her a harpsichord for here and she would sit and play for hours. Hours and hours and hours. It is like nails on a chalkboard as far as I'm concerned. Maybe I can smash it to pieces and box them up for delivery to Jonathan and Sarah. I'll do it myself too. Smashing that horrid instrument of torture to smithereens would feel good. Really good. I'm going to tell Tatiana to order a big fucking rubber mallet. First clear day we get, that damn thing goes outside and I'll break it apart. Definitely something to look forward to.

I am truly sorry I won't be seeing little Jonny or Athena anymore. They are cute kids. Athena is going to be a beauty despite her mother's mousy appearance, and she always makes me laugh. She reminds me a lot of Gigi's brother Nick, with her huge dark eyes and love of a good joke. Maybe I can amend their trusts so they'll have to see me? Or better yet, maybe Gigi will bring them for visits. She wouldn't want innocent children to be kept from their Grampy. Best if there is no paperwork—just their kindhearted grandmother making the case for maintaining the relationship.

And while Jonathan is a lost cause, Vivian is still my shining star. She's simply brilliant at everything she does. Right by my side during every crisis in the White House and now returning as CEO of the family business. I'd never admit it to anyone, but she is a better CEO than I ever was. I was great at expanding the businesses into a global conglomerate, but she knows how to run that kind of mega-enterprise day-to-day. From Shanghai to Santos and everything in between, she doesn't miss a thing and nothing rattles her.

It's something of a consolation that she is leading the company again. Jonathan doesn't like having his sister back in charge, but he knew it was coming either now or in four years. If he hadn't fucked up and I was still president, he'd have had four more years at the top. He has no one to blame but himself.

I think Jamie is coming by this weekend. It will be good to see him. Vivian's sending him to Hong Kong for a few years and I think he'll do well there. He's a lot like his mother, very pragmatic and kind of a chameleon, so the international side of the business is a good match for him. That's another thing about Vivian: she has a keen sense of who fits where.

I wonder how Margeaux is doing, anyway. I talked to her briefly right after the election when she called to say she was sorry I lost. She was great campaigning for me out on the West Coast. Raised a lot of Hollywood money too. I should've stuck it out with her; then I wouldn't have this Amber problem to deal with, or those twins. They don't even look like me. I know what the DNA test said, but I still have my doubts. I don't trust a thing connected to that fucking woman. I've really got to get moving on the divorce. She's probably downstairs scheming about how to grab more of my assets right now, unless she's on that damn treadmill. How can she spend so many hours on that thing every day? She must've logged enough miles to have circled the Earth three times by now!

Oh, thank God, here is my coffee. I feel like I am running on fumes. At the White House they always had a pot of my special beans brewing so I could have a fresh cup as soon as I asked for it. Here, *in my own fucking home*, it takes them forever to get it from the kitchen upstairs to my office. How is this so fucking hard for them? If Amber wasn't so stupid, she could whip this staff into shape and run a proper household. Gigi knew how to do it. She ran three households. She knew how to make them each feel like a home, too.

I wish my father had gotten on with Gigi. I know all he wanted was for me to have a partner like he had with my mother. They built that business together, and in many ways it was mother's vision that made it a success, but it was always clear to me that they had more of a business partnership than a love match. They respected each other—I'd even describe them as fond of each other—but I know for a fact it wasn't much more than that after I was born. Dad had a longtime girlfriend named Jenny. I'm guessing if I'd asked him, he would've admitted that he was in love with Jenny, not my mother. I've always wondered why he didn't get a divorce and marry Jenny, but I was afraid to ask him. Now I just assume it was to keep the business intact for me and to keep up appearances.

My parents were both very concerned with keeping up appearances. The moment they left the house, they became the image of the perfect couple. The world saw a couple who had it all: a successful business, social status, beautiful homes, a devoted son to carry on the business, and a loving marriage. Inside the house, all they talked to each other about was the business and me.

I think I loved Gigi's family almost as much as I loved her. They had family dinners where we all cooked together in their tiny kitchen and laughed until tears rolled down our faces. We laughed about everything. Her younger brother Nick was hilarious. Everybody hugged and kissed each other—all the time and for any reason. We talked about everything from Syracuse basketball to the fishing village the grandparents came from in Greece. At the end of the night, the goodbyes were prolonged and affectionate.

When Gigi came to New York, she found our family dinners to be completely different. We talked about the business before, during, and after dinner. People got up from the table to take calls. My parents frequently corrected her on her table manners, her outfit, or her view of the world, no matter how many times I asked them not to do it. My father sharply criticized my business performance in front of my wife, which humiliated me. The evening would end with us finding our own way out as my parents headed to their separate bedrooms. Gigi never complained, but I knew by the way she lay her head on my shoulder in the car as we rode home that she was hurt by their treatment of both of us.

Another question I should've asked my father is why he was so eager for me to divorce Gigi while he was so uninterested in divorcing my mother. Gigi had a lot to learn when we were first married, but she was a quick study and her warmth and kindness made everyone but my parents want to help her make the adjustment. My parents said she was too timid. She was provincial. She never had anything interesting to say. They complained that she couldn't bring anything to the family or the business because of her limitations. Wasn't I embarrassed by her?

She didn't go to college and she came from a small town, but over the years, she traveled with me and she read a lot. She could hold her own in almost any conversation by talking about the latest best seller, describing the beauty of a Japanese temple we once visited, or explaining how to cook octopus. In those days no one ate octopus and it was very exotic. I was never embarrassed by her. In fact, I was often very proud of her.

It's true she didn't like the spotlight except on the golf course, where she loved to win. She took the Women's Cup at her club down in Naples for five consecutive years after the divorce. Otherwise, Gigi hung back and avoided attention, even when it would've been good for the business to pose for a photo at a gala or let a magazine into our home to do a photospread. My mother was furious when *Architectural Digest* wanted to do a feature on the new Bridgehampton estate and Gigi wouldn't agree to do it. I could usually get her to do anything I wanted but she dug in her heels and wouldn't budge. She said it was our home and that was private space, not a business asset. My mother told her very pointedly that it was my house according to the prenup. The expression "if looks could kill" was likely coined describing an encounter like that one. They barely spoke for the next year but my mother had plenty to say about Gigi behind her back.

I see now that my parents just never gave her a chance. They wanted our marriage to fail and they wanted her out of our lives.

They had a very specific type of woman in mind for me and when I veered from the plan, they took it out on Gigi. Looking back on that time in my life, I realize my parents even tried to tempt me with other women, but I'm not a cheater. They switched tactics and tempted me with work and power and even fame. That proved to be an irresistible combination. It successfully pulled me away from my family, unlike the nieces of family friends who came to the office for informational interviews, or the debutante daughters of business associates who stopped by my parents in slinky little black dresses to say hello on their way to somewhere else while I was there to pick up something for the kids.

    When Dad died and I took over the businesses, the shit really hit the fan. Eventually, all the time away from home and the pressures of running the business broke us apart. My mother opened a bottle of champagne when I told her about the divorce. She said she'd been saving that special bottle for that exact moment. She said she knew I'd come to my senses one day. She said a lot of snarky things that night, but then she smiled at me and all was forgiven. Vivian has her smile and her way of lighting up the world with it.

Of course, I never did marry the girl of their dreams. Fortunately, they didn't know about the Suzy debacle. Dad was dead and my mother was in and out of reality as Alzheimer's ate away at her mind.

No more procrastinating: time to call Gigi. If she's not down in Naples, I might even get her out here in the next couple of days. If she says yes, I'll have Tatiana bring in the barber and spruce me up. I'm looking a little shaggy. And the cook can make lobster bisque; she always loved lobster bisque. She had it on our honeymoon for the first time and thought it was the most wonderful thing she'd ever eaten. Hearts of palm salad, too. That's another of her favorites. It'll be getting warm in Bermuda soon. Maybe we can go on a golf vacation this spring. Not sure how that will look as the divorce is announced, but if we make it clear it's platonic, it could be a positive for me. It's a good contrast: Gigi's classic, elegant style versus trashy piece of shit Amber. It plays nicely into the sympathy narrative I want to build post-divorce. Yes, Gigi is the key to figuring out where I go from here. This throbbing headache might stop if I get out of this cold, damp climate, too.

Postscript

From the other side of the door, the Secret Service agent heard a heavy thud and the breaking of china against the hardwood floor. She quickly but carefully entered the office to assess the situation, where she found him lying on the floor next to his worn leather wing chair by the massive picture window that looked out to the sea. She remembered him telling her it was his father's reading chair from the apartment where he grew up. There was a broken mug in pieces beside him and coffee spreading across the floor. His phone was lying a few feet away as if it had fallen with him and then slid. The agent checked for a pulse, but it was obvious that he was gone. He'd likely been gone before he even hit the ground. "The poor, miserable bastard," she muttered as she called her supervisor to start the chain of events that are triggered when a past president dies. "Gotham is down," she told him using the Secret Service code name. "I repeat, Gotham is down and out."

Amber was calm when they told her. He'd put on another twenty pounds since leaving Washington and was drinking too much coffee and too much beer. The thought that he might suffer a heart attack or stroke had crossed her mind more than once, but she knew better than to suggest he watch his diet or get some exercise. Now, her priority was protecting the boys as the house filled up with the many people tasked with managing the death of an ex-president, including her overbearing, controlling stepdaughter who would surely arrive as quickly as possible to run the show. But this time, Amber was happy to let Vivian take over. Soon, this would all be behind her.

Vivian told her mother, handed the hysterical woman over to her brother Jonathan, then headed out to Bridgehampton to be the point person for the family. Her husband told Allegra and Chad and sent them off to finish their homework, but instead they huddled together on Allegra's canopy bed trying to figure out what this all meant and what they were supposed to do. It was scary.

In the helicopter on her way to the Hamptons house, Vivian spoke to Margeaux and Jamie and the lawyers, and then she was briefed by the Secret Service agent in charge. The Secret Service was keeping the household staff under their watchful eyes to prevent press leaks. Upon her arrival, she informed the staff of the facts of the situation and instructed them about what was expected of them. She reminded them of the non-disclosure agreements they all signed upon their employment. She designated her office in the house as the family's command center, and from there she approved the announcement of his death on behalf of the family and spoke with selected and favored members of the press. She took the new president's condolence call on behalf of Amber and the family, and she made calls to extended family, friends, and business associates.

Vivian knew how Daddy would've wanted things to go in this situation, as she did in every situation. She knew she was the best person to handle all the arrangements, so she simply took the lead. There was no need to ask for permission. They all understood and expected her to step in and take charge, a pattern that had been established long ago.

Jonathan sat with his mother and they consoled each other, crying on and off for a couple of hours until they were exhausted. Sarah and the kids joined them and they all snuggled with Yaya on the pillowy sectional sofa in her den, telling Grampy stories.

Later they ordered pizza.

Notes

Yaya is a common Greek nickname for a grandmother that has several spelling variations. YiaYia is another popular spelling. I chose the spelling that most closely represented the english pronunciation. While it is not mentioned until the end of the book, Gigi is of Greek heritage.

The five Finger Lakes are located in upstate New York. It is a scenic region with many colleges and universities, including my alma mater Syracuse University. When Grampy was a college student, much of the area was still very rural. Today it remains picturesque but you will find tourist attractions such as breweries and vineyards with tasting rooms that would not have existed when Grampy was a student. Coming from Manhattan, this very different, rustic part of New York state would've felt alien to him and deepened his sense of isolation until he met Gigi.

Pacific Palisades is a hilly area on the westside of Los Angeles. When Grampy and Margeaux lived there it would've featured pretty Spanish style homes with pools – the California dream. It was a fashionable neighborhood but quieter and less showy than Beverly Hills.

Grampy and Suzy make their ill-fated trip to Las Vegas just as that city is transitioning away from original "Rat Pack" Vegas. The new, exotic hotels like The Luxor and The Mirage are opening and acts like Penn & Teller and Siegfried and Roy are the big draws. I imagined the stark contrast between old Vegas and the emerging over-the-top new Vegas subliminally agitated Grampy because he was still struggling with leaving behind his life as a family man and recreating himself as a public figure and a player.

Made in the USA
Middletown, DE
15 July 2024